THE MAJOR AND THE
MOUSEHOLE MICE

THE MAJOR AND THE
MOUSEHOLE MICE

by Jane Chelsea Aragon
illustrated by John O'Brien

SIMON AND SCHUSTER BOOKS FOR YOUNG READERS
Published by Simon & Schuster Inc., New York

SIMON AND SCHUSTER BOOKS FOR YOUNG READERS
Simon & Schuster Building, Rockefeller Center
1230 Avenue of the Americas, New York, New York 10020

10 9 8 7 6 5 4 3 2 1

Library of Congress Cataloging-in-Publication Data. Aragon, Jane Chelsea. The major
and the mousehole mice / written by Jane Chelsea Aragon; illustrated by John O'Brien.
p. cm. Summary: When a retired major and his wife move into a mouse-infested
cottage, the major decides to teach the mice a lesson with unexpected results. [1. Mice—
Fiction.] I. O'Brien, John, 1953- ill. II. Title. PZ7.A66Maj 1990 89-32516 [E]—
dc20 CIP AC ISBN 0-671-68853-7

To my sister Amy, who knew Lightfoot personally
J.C.A.

To Terese
J. O'B.

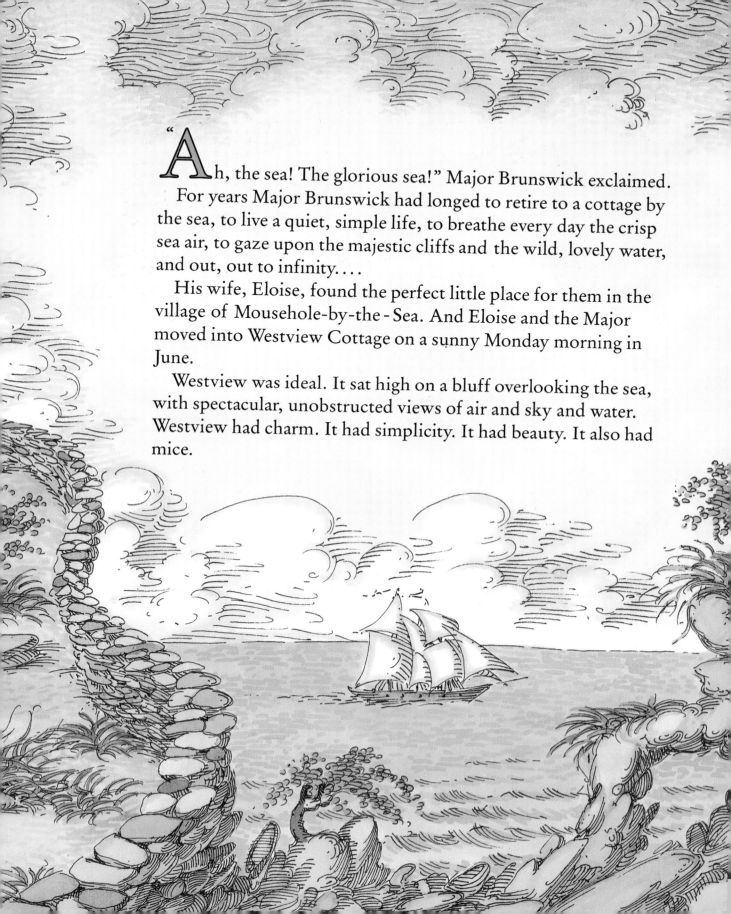

"Ah, the sea! The glorious sea!" Major Brunswick exclaimed.

For years Major Brunswick had longed to retire to a cottage by the sea, to live a quiet, simple life, to breathe every day the crisp sea air, to gaze upon the majestic cliffs and the wild, lovely water, and out, out to infinity....

His wife, Eloise, found the perfect little place for them in the village of Mousehole-by-the-Sea. And Eloise and the Major moved into Westview Cottage on a sunny Monday morning in June.

Westview was ideal. It sat high on a bluff overlooking the sea, with spectacular, unobstructed views of air and sky and water. Westview had charm. It had simplicity. It had beauty. It also had mice.

Well, what respectable old cottage doesn't? The previous occupant of Westview, a Miss Craddock, had dealt quite well with the situation. She simply tossed a wedge of cheese or a biscuit into the little hole in the corner of the pantry every now and then, and the mice were content.

In this way, Miss Craddock and her finches had lived for years side by side with the mice: Simon and Emma, their daughter Penelope, and Lightfoot, their son. The mice kept to their part of the cottage—their part being the passageways under the floors and between the walls—and Miss Craddock kept to hers—her part being the rest. The mice retained the use of the little secret room under the pantry, which had always been their domain simply because none of the occupants of Westview had ever discovered it. (This was where the mice put up their out-of-town relations when they came to visit for the holidays.)

In keeping to this arrangement, Miss Craddock had never even seen the mice in person, except once when her cousin's cat stayed over, and Lightfoot brought everybody out into the sitting room to have a look at him.

But now Miss Craddock had moved out, and Major Brunswick had moved in, and as they say, nothing stays the same forever.

Simon and Emma had taken the children to visit relatives, and they had had no knowledge of an impending change in tenancy. When they returned, things were not as they had left them.

First, they noticed that the hole in the pantry had been plugged up, and they wondered how Miss Craddock intended to get cheese and biscuits to them. Then Penelope remarked that the finches were awfully quiet. But when they saw a large, roundish man wearing lots of medals inspecting the roses in the flower garden, it dawned on them that Miss Craddock and the finches were no longer there.

Who was this chubby resident? The mice all had different theories. Simon was certain that the man with all the medals was in charge of a military unit, and had moved into Westview Cottage to guard the coastline. Emma said no, that couldn't be, because the only other person at Westview was a lady who was busy hanging curtains and polishing silver, and Emma didn't think she would be much help on a military maneuver.

Penelope hoped that her father was right, though, because with a lot of soldiers around, there was bound to be lots of edible trash.

But Lightfoot said it was all speculation, and he marched right outside to survey the situation. He ran through the garden and across the cobbled walkway, and then ran directly up to the Major, whereupon Major Brunswick lost his reason. He jumped up and down, and uttered uncalled-for remarks not at all befitting a major, and then he ran to get the broom.

Lightfoot's report to his family was as follows: an insane man
had put on a terrific show in the flower garden, and he feared
Westview had been turned into an asylum.

Poor Miss Craddock, poor little finches. They had been so happy there. It was a shame they had to leave. But it was understandable that they didn't want to share the premises with lunatics.

When Major Brunswick calmed down, Eloise was able to get the story out of him.

"Mice!" he said. "Westview is...infested! I shall have to capture them! Trap them all!"

Eloise was a different sort of person than her husband, and she had nothing at all against mice. She only asked, "Where do they find food?"

"Food, Eloise? You're worried about them starving to death?" Major Brunswick howled. "Would you like to bake them little cakes? Or little meat pies so they won't starve?"

Eloise had learned long ago that when the Major was in one of these moods, it was best just to go and hang some curtains. So that was what she did.

But Major Brunswick went straight to his study and searched through his books for information. He set to work at once.

As the sea air wafted through the window, Major Brunswick built a little cage with a door. Inside the cage was a plate, on which the Major placed a bit of cheese. When one of the little

creatures entered the cage and attempted to snatch the cheese, the door would slam shut, and then Major Brunswick could simply take the contraption out for a drive, and deposit the unwanted rodent in a meadow.

It was truly unfortunate that when Penelope wandered outside that evening, she scurried through an open window into the sitting room. All she wanted to do was to look around. She was curious to see how Eloise was fixing up the place—the curtains, the needlepoint chairs, the little statues on the mantelpiece.

Penelope had some furniture, too. It was dollhouse furniture, which she had inherited from a rich aunt. Of course, the needlepoint design was only painted on Penelope's little chair, and one leg was slightly broken, which made sitting difficult. But she had a doll's four-poster bed and fancy curtains that Emma had made from Miss Craddock's sewing scraps. And, of course, there was Penelope's treasure—her doll-sized violin.

Even though the violin had only one string, it added an air of elegance to family celebrations and holiday gatherings.

But Penelope was young, and not wise to the ways of the world. And, when she saw the cage in the sitting room, she ran in without thinking, grabbed the cheese, and the door slammed shut behind her.

Bewildered, Penelope sat for hours in the dark room. She was too upset to eat.

Emma became worried when Penelope didn't return, and Lightfoot set out to find his sister. Knowing how fond Penelope was of decorating, he went straight to the sitting room, where he found his frightened sister sitting in the mousetrap.

Lightfoot couldn't get the cage open. Penelope was very downcast. She didn't want to be separated from her family. Lightfoot wanted to do something to cheer her up, so he hurried downstairs and got Penelope's violin.

Penelope was so delighted to have her treasure, she nearly forgot her serious predicament. But at that moment the door opened and Major Brunswick came in, and although Lightfoot wanted to stay with Penelope, she convinced him that their mother couldn't bear the loss of two children in one night, and Lightfoot returned downstairs.

Early the next morning, Lightfoot had the brainstorm of watching from the roof as the Major's car drove off, so they were able to determine his general direction. Then, the family set out to find Penelope.

After what felt like hours, they heard violin music in the field beyond. It was the unmistakable sound of Penelope's one-string violin! There sat Penelope, entertaining the grasshoppers with her music.

Emma hugged her so tightly that Penelope could hardly breathe!

Once they were safely back at Westview, the mice had a family meeting. It was decided that Lightfoot would be the one to go out at night and get food for the family.

Lightfoot wasn't musical, like Penelope, but he had other talents. Night after night, to Major Brunswick's consternation, Lightfoot retrieved the bait from the mousetrap, and delivered it to his waiting family. He didn't trip the trap once. Peanut butter, jam, biscuits, gourmet cheeses, everything the Major left on the little plate was gone in the morning.

Major Brunswick became more and more frustrated. One morning, he actually saw Lightfoot escaping with some sweet sausage between his teeth. Major Brunswick was just about ready to burst, he was so furious. He'd had an exemplary career in the military, and he had medals to prove it. He'd fought in wars, vanquished enemies. And now he was being outwitted by a mouse! It was humiliating.

Eloise was leaving to visit her sister, and Major Brunswick would be alone for a month, during which time he could trap mice to his heart's content.

Unfortunately, shortly after Eloise's departure, Major Brunswick made a serious mistake. While looking for the mice, the Major pushed a bit too hard on a cabinet door in the pantry, and, before he knew it, he found himself tumbling down into the little secret room below.

He landed right in the middle of a family celebration, featuring Penelope on violin, and her cousin Cecile on pianoforte.

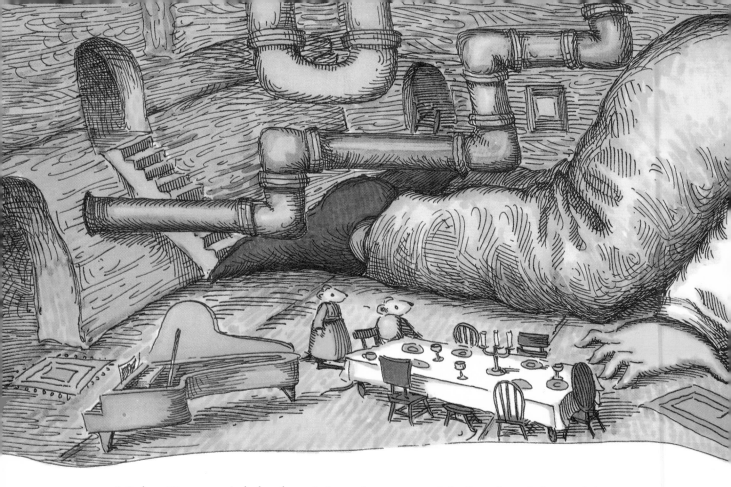

Major Brunswick had a vicious bump on his forehead from his nasty fall. Emma applied compresses, while the other relatives looked on with concern. Only Lightfoot was reserved. He hadn't forgotten the terrified look in Penelope's eyes the night she had been captured, and he held Major Brunswick responsible.

When he came to, the Major did several things. First, he screamed. Then he stamped his feet and shouted, "Get out!" to the mice. And then, he pointed to his medals.

"I'll have you know," Major Brunswick boasted, "that I am one of the most decorated military men in this country! I have wiped out entire battalions of invaders almost single-handedly!"

The mice were impressed, but they didn't see why they should be the ones who had to leave, when Major Brunswick was the obvious intruder.

But Major Brunswick couldn't leave, because the secret
passage only worked in one direction. There was no way for him
to get out until Eloise returned and rescued him from above.

"I shall die here, alone," moaned Major Brunswick, "with no
one to console me but mice."

Well, the mice couldn't let him die. They knew what they had
to do. Bit by bit, the mice carried food down to the secret room
through a crack in the foundation. And in this way, they kept
Major Brunswick alive.

Lightfoot was still unhappy about this arrangement, but
Emma took the opportunity to discuss with Lightfoot the
importance of forgiveness, and eventually he came around.

Weeks passed. As waves crashed against the cliffs and the sun warmed the dark beauty of the coastline, Major Brunswick spent his days nibbling on cheese bits with four companionable mice.

Major Brunswick missed Eloise terribly while he was trapped in the little room. Now he knew how Penelope must have missed her family when she had been captured. Penelope knew exactly how the Major was feeling, and she tried to cheer him up by serenading him on her violin.

Major Brunswick felt ashamed. The very mice he had been so determined to trap were now saving his life. He was so grateful to them for all their kindness, he gave each one a medal.

After what seemed like an eternity, Eloise returned from her sister's after a lovely stay. She was tired from her journey, and at first she disregarded the unusual knocking noises coming from under the pantry. She thought it must be a pipe rattling, and made a note to call the plumber.

But then she heard a muffled voice and strange squeaky music coming from under the floorboards. And then, a little mouse scampered in with a note.

"My dearest Eloise," it said. "Rescue me! Push as hard as you can on the low cabinet in the pantry!" It was signed, "M.B."

Eloise gave the messenger mouse a piece of cheese, and then proceeded to do as the note instructed. She pushed with some difficulty, so when he finished his cheese, Lightfoot tried to help.

And when the cabinet swung open, the Major shouted with joy, and leaped up into the kitchen. He was followed by the mice.

"Eloise! My dearest love!" Major Brunswick cried with joy.

"Dear," she asked, "why are all these mice wearing medals? Have you started an army in the basement while I was away?"

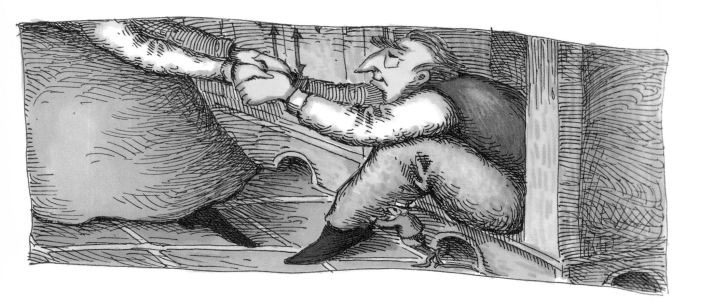

The Major sat with Eloise in front of the fireplace, and
recounted to her his entire ordeal. He related the mice's heroism
in detail. The mice all sat and listened, too. Eloise was astounded.
And from then on, it was agreed: the mice would remain at
Westview, with Eloise and the Major, as honored guests.